Paul Sellers
Alphabats®

Big Bubble
Adventure

GW01003516

TRANSWORLD PUBLISHERS LTD

LONDON • NEW YORK • TORONTO • SYDNEY • AUCKLAND

It was a beautiful way to
begin a day.

Bluebirds were singing,
bumble bees were buzzing and
the sun beamed into
the bedroom.

Big 'B' and Little 'b' sat up in
their bunk beds.

The sunlight was so bright,
they blinked and rubbed their eyes.

Then they bundled back the blankets, tumbled out of bed and stumbled into the bathroom.

Every morning, the Alphabats have a bath before breakfast.

"I'll run the bath, while you lay the table," said Big 'B'.

Little 'b' bounded down the stairs to put the breakfast things on the table.

Box of cereal... bottle of milk...
bowl of sugar...

brown bread and butter...
blackberry jam...

and a bunch of bananas!

"Be quick!" called Big 'B', squeezing the last drop of bubble bath from its bottle.

By the time Little 'b' had raced back to the bathroom, the bath was filled to the brim.

They both took off their
boots and climbed in.

"Scrub-a-dub-dub,
in the rub-a-dub tub!"
Little 'b' sang and scrubbed, while
Big 'B' blew bubbles.

"Oh boy! Look at THIS!" said Big 'B'.
"It must be the biggest bubble
there has ever been!"

They watched in amazement as
the bubble grew bigger and bigger...

...and BIGGER!

Before long, the bubble was above them, filling the bathroom like a giant balloon.

The Alphabats couldn't believe their eyes when, suddenly, the walls and ceiling parted...

Then the bath began to RISE!

Up... up... they floated, into the bright blue sky.

As the bubble balloon bobbed along on the breeze, Big 'B' and Little 'b' peeped over the edge of the bath.

Beneath them, they could see buildings, and trees full of blossom.

A stream of bright water
bubbled and babbled merrily
between two banks.

"Look! There's a brook!" cried Little 'b'.
"There's a brass band in
a bandstand!" spied Big 'B'.

They waved to a boy on a bus
and EVERYBODY waved back.

A barn, a bicycle, a bat and a ball. Big and little, they saw them all!

"There's a bakery!"
"There's a butcher's shop!"
"There's a builder's truck!"
They couldn't stop.

The Alphabats were having a wonderful time, but they were so busy looking down below that they did not see what was ABOVE them.

WHAM-BAM! BASH! BONK!

A flock of blackbirds with yellow beaks bumped into their bubble balloon!

Big 'B' and Little 'b' waved their
arms and shouted,
"Hey! Be careful!"
"You'll break it!"

But before they could shout again,
the bubble balloon burst...
BANG!

Then the bath began to FALL!

Down... down... tumbling down, out of the bright blue sky.

Big 'B' and Little 'b' trembled, expecting to SMASH into the ground!

As they waited for the CRASH, they could not bear to look. Then the bathtub landed...

SPLASH!

In the middle of the brook!

When the Alphabats opened their eyes, they both had a BIG surprise.

They were safe and happy and still afloat, bobbing along in their bubble bath BOAT!

"Where shall we go?" asked Big 'B'.
"I'm hungry!" said Little 'b'.

So the Alphabats paddled back home for breakfast.

BIG BUBBLE ADVENTURE
0 552 528994

First published in Great Britain by Transworld Publishers Ltd, 1995

Transworld Publishers Ltd,
61-63 Uxbridge Road, London W5 5SA
Published in Australia by Transworld Publishers (Australia) Pty Ltd
15-25 Helles Avenue, Moorebank, NSW 2170
and in New Zealand by Transworld Publishers (NZ) Ltd
3 William Pickering Drive, Albany, Auckland

Made and printed in Great Britain